EAST SIDE STORY

by Bonnie Bader

SILVER MOON PRESS
NEW YORK

EAST SIDE STORY
by Bonnie Bader
Copyright © 1993 by Kaleidoscope Press
First paperback edition 1995

For information contact
Silver Moon Press
New York, New York
(800) 874-3320

First Edition
Designed by John J. H. Kim
Cover Illustration by Nan Golub
Printed in the United States of America

Library of Congress Cataloging-in-Publication Data

Bader, Bonnie, 1961-
    East Side Story / by Bonnie Bader. -- 1st ed.
    p. cm. -- (Stories of the States)
    Summary: A young girl and her older sister, working in the Triangle Shirtwaist factory, an early twentieth-century sweatshop on the Lower East Side of New York City, join a protest to try to improve the miserable working conditions.
    ISBN 1-881889-22-X (hardcover): $13.95
    ISBN 1-881889-71-8 (paperback): $5.95
    1. Triangle Shirtwaist Company--Juvenile Fiction. [1. Triangle Shirtwaist Company--Fiction. 2. Factories--Fiction. 3. Labor disputes--Fiction. 4. Strikes and lock-outs--Fiction. 5. New York (N.Y.)--History--1898-1951--Fiction. 6. Sisters--Fiction.] I. Title. II. Series.
PZ7.B1377Eas 1993
[Fic]--dc20
                                          93-1919
                                          CIP

STORIES OF THE STATES

# TABLE OF CONTENTS

CHAPTER ONE
"We Pay You to Work, Not to Waste Time"

"And just where do you think you're going, young lady?" a shrill voice called out. Eleven-year-old Rachel Boganovitch quickly turned around and found herself standing face-to-face with Mrs. Stein, one of the supervisors at the Triangle Shirtwaist Company where she worked. Rachel's heart began to beat fast. The last thing she wanted was to be in trouble with this unpleasant, suspicious woman.

"What have you been doing?" Mrs. Stein asked, her eyes narrowing into tiny slits. She was standing where she always stood—at the back of the crowded, stuffy room where she could observe everything and everyone with her steely eyes. Eight long wooden sewing tables filled almost the entire room. Young girls and women sat closely, side by side, around the tables, hunched over the sewing machines. They were stitching together sections of the close-fitting blouses, called shirt-waists.

"I was just using the toilet," Rachel answered meekly. "My stomach is upset."

"That is not the truth, young lady, and you know it," Mrs. Stein said with a scowl.

Rachel's heart beat even faster; she was definitely in trouble now. She looked down and nudged a piece of dirty fabric with the toe of her boot. Rachel knew better than to leave her work for too long. The supervisors constantly watched the workers. They weren't allowed to spend too much time in the bathroom, and were never given breaks. They were not even supposed to talk to each other.

"I'll have none of your nonsense," Mrs. Stein continued, stamping her foot. "It should only take you three minutes to use the toilet, and you were gone eight. I timed you! You should be trimming the garments," Mrs. Stein continued, throwing up her hands in disgust, "not wasting time."

"It won't happen again," Rachel promised, hanging her head.

"And no back talk!" Mrs. Stein shouted. "Now get to work."

With that, she pushed Rachel toward one of the crowded sewing tables.

Thud!

Rachel gasped and looked down at the floor. Something had fallen out of her skirt and now lay at her feet.

"What have we here?" Mrs. Stein said, bending down. "A book? So this explains why you were gone so long," she said with a sneer.

Rachel couldn't believe her terrible luck. She was sure she had tied the book securely to her waist under her petticoat. But the shove from Mrs. Stein must have jarred it loose.

"*The Adventures of Tom Sawyer*," Mrs. Stein read the title. "Well, young lady, we do not pay you to read. And you will learn that lesson when you receive your pay at the end of the week."

Rachel gulped. She could not afford to lose any of her wages. Every cent of the $3.50 a week she earned was desperately needed at home.

Mrs. Stein flashed an evil smile at Rachel. Then she turned and walked away, pounding her fist on the cover of the book.

"Can't take your nose out of the book, can you?" Rachel heard someone say.

She looked up and saw Amelia Russo, one of the seamstresses, laughing at her. Rachel felt the heat begin to rise from under her high-buttoned collar, and she knew her face had turned a bright shade of red. Why was Amelia always picking on her? Rachel was embarrassed enough that Mrs. Stein had yelled at her in front of everyone. Amelia was only making things worse. Rachel dug her feet into cracks between the floorboards, wishing she could create a big hole to crawl into and hide.

"Leave her alone!" Rachel heard her older sister Leah call out. Like Amelia, Leah worked as a sewing machine operator at the factory.

"Why must you always defend this little brat?" Amelia asked Leah in a nasty voice. "Can't she speak up for herself?"

Rachel glanced at her sister. It was true, Leah always did try to protect her. Leah was a fighter, and she never let anyone push her around. While Rachel appreciated her sister's support, sometimes she wished that Leah would just leave things alone.

"Speak up for what you think is right," Leah prodded her sister. "Remember what I always tell you: never let anyone push you around."

"Do I hear talking?" Mrs. Stein stood behind Rachel, her hands on her hips. "If I hear another word, you'll each find part of your wages missing this week! Now get back to work, girls!" Mrs. Stein shouted.

Rachel hurried over to one of the sewing tables and sat down on a low stool. When the sewing machine operators were finished making the shirtwaists, it was Rachel's job to take a pair of scissors and trim off the threads.

Rachel hated working at the Triangle Shirtwaist Company. She wished she could go to school with her two brothers. But instead, every morning, she and her sister would walk to the Triangle Factory, which was located in the Asch Building, at the corner of Washington Place and Greene Street in New York City. The top three floors of the ten-story building housed the Triangle Shirtwaist Company. The sisters would take the freight elevator up nine floors to the dark, dirty shop. The girls worked Monday through Saturday from seven-thirty in the morning until six-thirty at night when it wasn't busy, and until nine when there was a lot of work. Even though they worked longer hours during the busy season, they still received the same salary. There was no such thing as overtime pay at the Triangle Shirtwaist Company.

Five years ago Rachel and her family had come to America from Russia, hoping for a better life. It was now 1909, and things seemed worse than ever. They were told they would have freedom in America, which was true, but working at the Triangle Factory was oppressive. The doors were kept locked during the workday, and the windows couldn't be opened. Rachel shivered at the thought of the supervisors, like Mrs. Stein, who took note of every breath the workers took.

"We Pay You to Work, Not to Waste Time"

Rachel looked up for a moment at the women around her. They looked pale and weary from constant work. Black rings were etched under their eyes. Scowls seemed to be permanently planted on their faces. There was no fresh air in the factory, and beads of sweat trickled down the workers' faces on this hot September day. No wonder they called this place a sweatshop, Rachel thought.

Rachel lifted up a sleeve of the shirtwaist she was working on and quickly snipped the loose threads hanging from the seam. The rhythmic hum of the sewing machines was punctuated by the clip, clip, clip of her scissors.

She held up the scissors and tried to make out her reflection in the steel blades. Her dark hair hung around her face in damp ringlets, and her brown eyes were as round as coins. Her normally ruddy cheeks were smudged with dirt and soot.

Rachel wished she could look more like

her sister, Leah, who had straight jet black hair and bright blue eyes. Not only did Rachel not look like her sister, but their personalities couldn't be further apart. Leah was outspoken, while Rachel was quiet, often lost in her world of books.

Rachel sighed. She wished she could live like one of the wealthy characters in her books, wearing elegant new clothes and shiny shoes, and learning wonderful things in school.

Suddenly, a pair of rough hands jarred Rachel from her daydream. The shirtwaist she was working on was pulled away from her, and she was whisked into the air. The scissors fell to the floor with a clatter.

"Keep still, child," a raspy voice whispered in her ear.

The next thing Rachel knew, she was flung into one of the crates used to ship material in. Finished shirtwaists were thrown on top of her, and her world went dark.

CHAPTER TWO
"You Must Tell Me What Happened!"

Rachel lay quietly in the crate. She dared not make a sound. Carefully, she stretched out her leg. She hit something soft. It was another person! Slowly, she reached out her arm and felt fingers. Rachel grasped them tightly, and lay there with her eyes shut, listening to her own quick breathing.

After what seemed like hours, Rachel heard some rustling from above. She cracked open one eye, and a ray of light pierced her vision. The layers of shirtwaists were soon peeled away, and Rachel could again breathe the musty air of the sweatshop.

"Let's go, girls," Mrs. Stein called. "The visit from the building inspectors wasted enough of our time already. I don't need you to waste any more."

Rachel and about ten other children, some as young as eight, climbed shakily out of the crates. So, the inspectors were here again, Rachel thought, as she helped the smaller children from the crates. I wish they'd find us one day and close this whole place down. When the inspectors visited the shop, the supervisors would force all the children to hide in the crates because it was against the law for children as young as Rachel to work in the factory. Rachel remembered the first time she was thrown into one of the crates, and how frightened she had been. But now she was so used to the experience, she didn't even cry anymore.

The children all went back to their jobs—some snipping threads, some handing the fabric to the sewing machine operators. Rachel sighed as she returned to her job clipping loose threads. She wished she didn't have to work in this awful place. But her family counted on her earnings, small though they were.

Rachel's heart was heavy as she remembered her eleventh birthday. Papa had told her that she was now old enough to hold down a job. What a birthday present that had been! Rachel had loved school, and had received the best grades in the family. But that didn't matter, since she was a girl, and girls were not supposed to need an education. Papa had explained to her over and over that her two brothers, Daniel and Samuel, were the ones who belonged in school, because they were boys. Oh, how angry that had made Rachel, but she would never dare talk back to Papa. That was simply not allowed. Some day she'd go back to school. Somehow she'd find a way to do it.

Soon it was time to go home. Rachel stood up, stretched her aching body, and looked around for her sister. Leah wasn't sitting with the other sewing machine operators. Perhaps she had gone to use the toilet. Five minutes went by, but there was still no sign of her. The other workers had shut off the machines and left the factory. An eerie silence filled the shop. Suddenly a shrill voice broke the quiet.

"We run a shirtwaist factory here, not a boarding house," Rachel heard Mrs. Stein say. "Now get on home." And with that, she pushed Rachel toward the freight elevator.

Although Rachel was concerned about her sister, she did not want to get into any more trouble today. She was too weary and her head ached. Perhaps Leah was already outside.

She rang for the elevator, stepped in, and descended to the street level. The whoosh of fresh air that greeted her felt good. Rachel breathed deeply, and ran her fingers through her hair. If only I could live in the country, she thought. She looked down the block and saw the elegant Washington Square park. Somehow, it didn't belong near the dirty factory.

"Well, if it isn't Miss Bookworm," Rachel heard a boy call.

She looked across the street, and saw Antonio Russo, Amelia's younger brother, kneeling on the sidewalk shooting marbles with two other boys. Rachel quickly turned her face away from them.

"Aw, don't be a fraidy cat, Bookie." Antonio left his friends and crossed the street.

"Why don't you just leave me alone?" Rachel stammered.

"Because I like to tease you," Antonio said, pulling at one of Rachel's curls.

"Don't touch her, Antonio," one of his friends called. "Who knows what kind of disease you might pick up."

"Yes," Rachel said, "please don't touch me."

"What's the matter? You don't have your big sister here to defend you?" Antonio said, tossing a marble in the air. "I guess you'll just have to protect yourself."

Antonio was right, but Rachel was too timid to stand up for herself. Although she felt angry inside, she rarely showed it to others. Now Leah, on the other hand, would explode like a boiling pot of water. Rachel turned away from Antonio and headed down the street to look for her sister. It was getting late, and they had to get home.

"Go read a book!" Antonio called after her.

My book! Rachel thought. Mrs. Stein never returned the book she had taken away. Rachel ran back to the factory and tried the doors. They were locked. She banged on them with her fists.

"You Must Tell Me What Happened!"

Suddenly, the doors burst open, sending Rachel sprawling to the sidewalk. Behind her, she heard Antonio and his friends shout with laughter. She felt her neck get hot, and knew that for the second time that day her face had turned a bright red.

Rachel stood up and attempted to wipe the dirt from her dress. She saw Leah and several other women emerge from the building.

Leah walked up to Rachel and grabbed her arm. "Come on, Rachel, we'll be late getting home," she said.

"But where have you been?" Rachel asked. "I looked for you inside, but you weren't there. Then I waited outside, and Antonio Russo and his friends started bullying me."

"I have no time for your whining now, Rachel," Leah said.

"Leah, please tell me what happened," Rachel said, starting to worry. She knew something was wrong.

"Not now," Leah said firmly. She grabbed

Rachel's hand and pulled her toward home.

They walked in silence for several blocks, past rows of tenement buildings five to eight stories high. The fronts of the buildings were lined with fire escapes; washlines crisscrossed the dark alleys between buildings. Peddlers shouted their wares in front of their push-carts. Children ran and played in the streets, while their mothers hung from their tene-ment windows, gossiping and complaining about the heat. The most common language heard was Yiddish, but many other languages, including broken English, were also spoken.

What could have happened inside the fac-tory? Rachel wondered. She knew it must have been something bad, because Leah was very upset. Was the factory closing? They certainly couldn't afford to lose their jobs. Where would they find new work?

Finally, Rachel couldn't keep her thoughts to herself anymore. She tugged on her sister's hand, and stopped walking. "Leah, you must tell me what happened."

"You want to know what happened?" Leah shouted. "I really don't think you want to hear it!"

Rachel shrank back against a lamppost. Passersby stopped and turned toward Leah.

"What are you all staring at?" Leah yelled at the people. "Go mind your own business."

"Leah," Rachel said softly. "Please calm down."

"You're right. I'm sorry." She took a deep breath, put her arm around Rachel's shoulder, and began to explain.

"They told us there will be less business from now on. Something to do with a change in fashions. They said that fewer people will be placing orders for the clothes we make," Leah started.

"So they want to cut your hours?"

"Not exactly," Leah said. "They told us that for the time being there was no more work."

"I don't understand," Rachel said, but she really did. Leah was right — she didn't want to hear what her sister was saying.

"Rachel, I've been fired!"

CHAPTER THREE
"They're Picketing the Shop"

"Fired!" Rachel exclaimed. She was looking right at her sister Leah.

"That's right, I've been fired," Leah said. "Now can we please go home? I've got to make some plans."

Soon they reached their tenement on Eldridge Street in a Jewish neighborhood on the Lower East Side, a poor section of the city. Rachel pushed open the door to the run-down building, and they climbed the five flights of dark stairs to their apartment. On the way up, Rachel could hear the whir of sewing machines, babies crying, and pots and pans clattering behind closed doors. She had to step over several children playing on the landings and on the steps as she went along.

Slowly, Rachel opened the door to their apartment. She wondered what her father's reaction would be when he heard that Leah had been fired.

"Where have you girls been?" their mother cried. Her dark hair was pulled back in a bun, and her blue eyes looked tired. She was sitting in the front room, behind a sewing machine, with scraps of fabric and newly sewn trousers and shirts strewn about. "I haven't had time to finish making supper. Mr. Elowitz needs these trousers first thing in the morning."

"We had to stay late at work," Leah said, pushing past Rachel and walking into the tiny living room.

"I need the potatoes peeled for supper, and the table set," their mother said, easing the trousers through the sewing machine. "Papa will be home any minute."

"Yes, Mama," Rachel said. "I'll help."

She walked through the living room where her two dark-haired, slender brothers—fourteen-year-old Daniel and eight-year-old Samuel—were studying. Four-year-old Hannah was rolling a spool of thread across the floor.

"Rachel!" Hannah cried, running up and hugging her older sister. Her blonde curls bounced as she ran, and her blue eyes shone brightly.

"Hush, Hannah," Daniel called. "We're doing our homework."

Rachel looked at her brothers with envy. They never had to go to work or prepare supper or clean the house. All they had to do was go to school and keep up with their studies. It just wasn't fair.

Rachel sighed, picked up the spool of thread, and handed it to her little sister. Then she turned and headed into the kitchen. Leah was already there, opening a small metal box.

"What are you doing?" Rachel asked.

"It's none of your concern, Rachel," Leah answered quickly. "And not a word of this to anyone. Understand?" She pulled out a pile of papers, shoved the box in a corner, and covered it with a bolt of fabric.

Rachel nodded, and went to the sink to wash her hands. She lit the flame under the large pot of soup on the stove. Then she pulled out another pot, filled it with water, and set it on the stove to boil. After peeling the potatoes, she placed them in the boiling water.

Next, she cleared the scarred wooden table and laid a much-mended white cloth over it. As she put seven place settings on the table, Rachel remembered how it was when they first arrived in America from Russia.

Then they all had to share the same knife and fork. She wondered if they would have to sell these utensils now that Leah was out of work.

The front door slammed. "Papa!" Rachel heard Hannah call. Papa was home from the shop where he worked as a tailor. Quickly, Leah hid the papers.

"Hello, Hannah," Papa said, as he greeted her with a hug. "Is my supper ready?" Papa's voice boomed.

"Yes, Papa." Leah ran from the kitchen to greet him.

"Daniel, Samuel," Leah heard her father say. "How was school today? Are you still getting good grades?"

"Yes, Papa," the boys answered.

"Hello, Papa," Rachel said as her father entered the kitchen.

He nodded at his middle daughter with a tired smile, and stroked his long, dark beard. Then he walked over to the sink to wash his hands, and sat down at the head of the table.

Once the entire family was seated, Mama served Papa first. She gave him the biggest bowl of soup, the largest potato, and the thickest slab of bread. Papa works hard, Mama often told them. He needs to keep up his strength.

"How was your day?" Mama asked Papa when everyone had helped themselves and had started eating.

"That crazy Mrs. Mendelsohn came into the shop and demanded that we have her husband's trousers finished by tomorrow, and Mr. Kaufman, one of the tailors, refused. And do you know what happened to him? He was fired! Imagine that!" Papa banged his fist on the table.

Mama shook her head in disbelief.

Leah did not mention that she had been fired, too.

Later that night, after the kitchen had been cleaned, and everyone was in bed,

Rachel climbed out onto the fire escape. This was her private place, a world of her own. Sometimes she would take her brothers' schoolbooks out here, and study them. But tonight, she just wanted to be alone and think.

What would happen to their family now that Leah had lost her job? Rachel wondered. Papa worked very hard, but his wages were too low to support a family of seven. They desperately needed all the extra money they could get. How would Papa react when he heard the news? She couldn't think of any answers to her questions. A dog howled — a pitiful howl. Rachel opened the window, climbed into the kitchen, which also served as a bedroom for Leah and her, and crawled into bed.

The next morning, Rachel felt someone shaking her. She sat up with a jolt. "What..."

Leah clasped a hand over her mouth. Rachel rubbed her eyes and saw that her sister was already dressed. In her hands was a newspaper.

"They lied to us," Leah began.

"What are you talking about?" Rachel asked.

"There's an advertisement in the paper asking for shirtwaist operators."

"Perhaps it's for another factory," Rachel said, yawning.

"No," Leah said. "It says it right here." She showed the paper to her sister. "Triangle Shirtwaist Company. Now hurry and get dressed." Leah pulled the blanket off her sister. "We're going to the factory."

Rachel didn't know what her sister had planned, and she was afraid to ask.

When they arrived at the factory, Rachel saw a group of women standing outside the doors. They were holding signs and shouting.

"Give us a fifty-two-hour work week!" one woman called out.

We need more fire escapes, one of the signs

read.

"What's going on?" Rachel wanted to know.

"They're picketing the shop," Leah answered.

"Does that mean we can't go in?" Rachel asked.

"Yes, Rachel, it does," Leah said. "I agree with these women that we have certain rights as workers. Since our employers don't see it the same way, we've decided it's time to do something to force them to change their minds. We have the right to a shorter work week, fair pay, and safe working conditions. And we won't go back to work until we get those things. We also plan on stopping any-one who tries to go into the factory."

"But I have to report for work. Our fami-ly needs the money," Rachel protested.

"Are you crazy, Rachel?" Leah said. "I just told you—no one can go in there!"

Rachel's head started to spin. Not go to

work? Things at home would be bad enough without Leah's pay. They couldn't survive if Rachel didn't work, either.

"No, Leah. I won't listen to you and your wild ideas," Rachel said. She knew it was the first time she had ever opposed her sister, but she couldn't let Leah order her around now. This was too important.

Leah stared open-mouthed at her sister. But before she could say anything, Rachel ran for the factory door.

"The shop is closed!" someone shouted at Rachel.

"Strikebreaker!" another person called.

"Traitor!" a young girl yelled, and pushed Rachel to the pavement.

Rachel held out her hands to break her fall. She bit her lip to hold back the yelp of pain as the skin was ripped from her palm.

"I told you not to go in there!" Leah cried, as Rachel was getting to her feet.

"Sorry," Rachel mumbled, tears filling her

eyes. She realized now that she should have listened to her sister.

"Go stand across the street and wait for me," Leah ordered.

Trembling, Rachel crossed the street and watched the crowd. Her sister joined in the shouting, and she and the other women tried to prevent anyone from entering the factory.

Soon, Rachel saw a group of tough-looking men and women approach the women who were picketing. Were they going to force the women to go back to work? Rachel wondered. But the newcomers just shouted back at the demonstrators. Rachel's heart began to pound as the volume became louder, the words more violent. A few thugs began shoving the women. Screams pierced the air. Sirens howled, and a police car pulled up, followed by a paddy wagon. Rachel was terrified. What was happening?

She shimmied up a lamppost to get a better view. There was total chaos. She couldn't find Leah. Would her sister be hurt in the angry crowd? Suddenly, using their sticks, the police began pulling the women out of the crowd. Then they shoved them into the paddy wagon. Rachel couldn't believe the terrible scene in front of her.

She thought she caught a glimpse of Leah's black hair and powder blue dress. Could it be? Yes! Leah was being led away by the policemen.

Her sister had been arrested!

CHAPTER FOUR
"My Sister Is in Trouble"

Rachel slid down from the lamppost and raced over to the paddy wagon. The last woman was being pushed in, and the doors were slammed shut.

"Leah!" Rachel cried, banging her fists frantically on the metal doors.

"Calm down, child," a woman said, gently pulling Rachel away from the car.

"But my sister's in there," Rachel sobbed.

"Don't worry, dear. She's doing the right

thing," the woman said, patting Rachel on the head.

The police wagon pulled away, leaving a cloud of smoke in Rachel's face. The fumes made her cough, and made her eyes sting. She squeezed her eyes shut, forcing a few dirty tears to make their way down her face.

Finally, the crowd cleared and the sirens faded. Rachel stood alone in the middle of the street and stared after the paddy wagon. She was numb. What could she do now? How could she help her sister? All she knew was that she had to do something—and fast.

Rachel spit on her palms, wiped off the dried blood from her fall, took a deep breath, and ran home.

Fortunately, when she arrived at the apartment, no one was there—she hadn't thought of an explanation to give her mother. She raced into the kitchen, took out the tin box that her sister had opened the night before, and pulled out the pile of papers.

"My Sister Is in Trouble"

"International Ladies' Garment Workers' Union, Local 25," Rachel read. Things were starting to make sense. Leah must have been fired because she joined the union.

A union would help the workers at the Triangle Shirtwaist Company get what they wanted. If the workers were united, it would be hard for the factory owners to hire other workers who were not in the union. Maybe then they would have to give in to the demands for labor reform. But surely it was dangerous to go behind the owners' backs and join a union. And her parents would probably object if they found out. No wonder Leah had hidden the papers.

Suddenly, Rachel heard the front door creak open. Mama was home! Quickly, Rachel gathered up the papers and slipped out onto the fire escape. She shivered—not so much from the sudden chill in the air, but from thinking about the events that had occurred so far that day.

"Hurry up, Hannah," Rachel heard her mother call. "I just came back to fetch a pair of trousers. I don't have time to wait for you now."

"But, Mama," Hannah wailed.

"Not now, Hannah." The front door slammed.

Rachel breathed a sigh of relief. She climbed back through the window, sat down on a chair, and looked through the papers. If Leah had them, she must be one of the organizers of the strike. Rachel skimmed through several pages of notes about joining the union, but none of the information seemed helpful. She was starting to get desperate. There must be something in here that I can use to help Leah, Rachel thought.

Then she came across a list of names and addresses of some of the girls who worked at the factory. Perhaps she could go to one of them for help. But, as she read the names, Rachel realized that most of these girls had been arrested, too.

Rachel's head began to ache, but she didn't want to give up hope. She was almost at the end of the list when she was surprised to see another familiar name. No, she thought. This can't be right. But there it was, written clearly in black ink: Amelia Russo.

Rachel thought that this had to be some sort of mistake. Her sister would never join a group that had Amelia Russo as a member. Besides, Amelia wasn't even at the demonstration today. She was probably inside the factory sitting at her sewing machine and laughing at all the foolish women outside.

Still, this was her only hope to help her sister. She must talk to Amelia.

Rachel left her apartment and headed in the direction of Mulberry Street, the Italian neighborhood where the Russos lived. She had never been to this neighborhood: Jews stayed in their neighborhood, and Italians stayed in theirs. Besides, to get to Mulberry

Street, she would have to cross the Bowery, a dangerous place.

Rachel checked the street signs as she walked: Forsyth, Chrystie, Bowery, Elizabeth, Mott. First she passed pushcart peddlers and children playing street games, like tag and roll-the-hoop. Then she came to the Bowery, with its many noisy and crowded saloons. Shabbily dressed men were everywhere. Some of them were lying on the sidewalks and some were crouching in doorways.

Finally, she reached Mulberry Street. Rachel looked up at the tenements that lined the streets. She was surprised to see that this neighborhood didn't look much different from hers. The pushcart peddlers shouted out the prices of their goods; children shouted and played games in the street; and women bustled along, carrying baskets filled with fresh fruit and vegetables.

Rachel checked the address she had written down on a piece of paper, and then looked up at the building in front of her. A boy sat on the fire escape, a cap pulled over his eyes, his knees hugged into his chest. In his hands, he held a book.

"Excuse me," Rachel called up to the boy.

The boy pushed his cap back and looked down at Rachel. She was shocked! The boy sitting on the fire escape reading a book was Antonio Russo! Her first impulse was to run away. But she had made it this far and she was determined to speak to Amelia.

Antonio squinted. "What are you doing here?" he asked.

"I've come to see your sister," Rachel answered boldly.

Antonio stood. "Come on up." He lowered the ladder to the fire escape and motioned for Rachel to climb up.

"So, what do you want?" Antonio asked when Rachel had reached the fire escape.

"I said, I came to see your sister," Rachel repeated.

Antonio shrugged. "Amelia!" he called, sticking his head inside the window. "You have a visitor."

"Who is it?" Amelia asked.

"Rachel Boganovitch, from the factory," Antonio said.

"Tell her I'm sick," Amelia said.

"Oh, please, Amelia," Rachel blurted out. "I must see you. My sister is in trouble."

"Oh, all right," Amelia said after a few seconds. "You can come in."

Rachel climbed in the window. The kitchen was small and cluttered with pots and pans. Amelia was sitting in the living room on an unmade bed. Her long, dark hair was pulled back into a braid, and she was still wearing her nightgown.

"Leah has been arrested," Rachel started to explain.

"And what makes you think I can help?" Amelia said.

"Because I saw your name on one of

Leah's lists," Rachel answered. "Whatever she's involved in, you're involved in it, too."

"Go on and tell her the truth, Amelia," Antonio said.

Rachel couldn't believe it. Antonio Russo was actually helping her? Perhaps he was just being an annoying younger brother. Whatever the case, Rachel was glad he had spoken up.

Amelia hung her head and sighed. "All right, Rachel," she said. "I'll help you. I really wanted to be there today, to show those owners they couldn't push us around. But my father forbade me to go. He said I was enough of an embarrassment to the family now that I had been fired. He wouldn't hear of me taking part in any sort of demonstration.

"But I realize I can't just sit here," Amelia continued. "I'll go to the union to find out what happened to the women who were arrested. Don't worry, Rachel, the union will get the bail money for your sister and the other girls. Leah will be home before night-fall."

"Oh, thank you," Rachel exclaimed.

"Now run along," Amelia said, getting up from her bed.

Rachel climbed back onto the fire escape. Antonio was perched there, reading a book. She looked closely at the title: *The Adventures of Tom Sawyer.*

"What's the matter?" Antonio asked. "You didn't think I could read?"

"I just..." Rachel started.

"Here," Antonio said, throwing the book at Rachel. "I've read it already."

Rachel was at a loss for words. She decided not to tell him it was the same book she had dropped on the floor of the factory when Mrs. Stein had scolded her. "Thanks," she mumbled, tucking the book under her arm.

Knowing Leah would be safe now, Rachel left Antonio's neighborhood and headed over to Hester Street to buy some herring for supper. Around her, men, women, and children were shouting in Yiddish, Russian, and broken English. People hurried past her, eager to buy their groceries and return home.

But Rachel did not notice the crowd. She didn't seem to hear the shouts, the yells, the constant noise. She was thinking about all the events of that day—about how proud her sister would be of her for helping her, about how proud she was of herself. She was also thinking about what lay ahead for her family. Without the money she and Leah earned, times would be tough. Yet, though she couldn't say why, Rachel felt that things would be all right—that somehow they'd manage.

CHAPTER FIVE
"It Looks Like We've Found a Friend"

"**H**urry up with those trousers, Rachel," her mother called to her. Rachel carefully pulled the black pants from the sewing machine and handed them to her mother.

"I have to run over to Mr. Hess's," Mrs. Boganovitch said, as she opened the front door. "Please start hemming the brown dress."

Rachel sighed. It had been two months

since the Triangle Shirtwaist Company workers had gone on strike. Surprisingly, Rachel's
parents supported the strike, and Leah's work
with the union. Now Leah was too busy helping to promote the union and working with
the strikers to look for another job. But
Rachel was able to help her mother with the
sewing, and that brought in some extra business. Still, it wasn't enough to make ends
meet.

Rachel looked around the crowded living
room that had now become the sewing room,
as well as her brothers' bedroom. Last month,
the family had decided to rent out the front
room, where Mama used to do the sewing, to
a boarder. So Mrs. Boganovitch moved her
sewing machine into the living room, pulled
out the feather bed she had brought from
Russia, and made a little chair and table from
an old barrel and some pieces of scrap wood.

They rented the room to the first person
who came to see it, a young man named Ivan

Goldstein. Ivan worked for the Daily Forward, a popular Yiddish newspaper. Rachel often heard her father grumble about Ivan's politics, but the rent money he paid helped the family survive. And Ivan and Leah seemed to get along very well. Ivan took an interest in the strike and advised Leah whenever he had a spare moment.

As Rachel sat sewing and daydreaming, the front door burst open. "Rachel!" a voice called.

Rachel looked up and saw Ivan Goldstein standing in the doorway. His dark hair fell over his eyes, and he was missing a button on his shabby gray jacket.

"What is it, Ivan?" Rachel asked.

"You must come quickly," Ivan said breathlessly. "Your sister needs you."

Rachel jumped up from her chair. "Has something happened to Leah? Is she in trouble?"

Ivan shook his head. "No. She just needs

your help with a little..." He paused. "A little project. I'm working on it too, but she needs all the help she can get."

Rachel looked down at the dress she was working on. She knew that her mother would expect it to be finished by the time she returned home. Still, she had been sitting in the house all day, and it would be nice to get outside.

"Let me just finish this hem, and I'll go with you," Rachel said.

Ivan led Rachel over to the Garden Cafeteria on East Broadway. Leah and the other union organizers spent a lot of time there. Since workers at only a few factories were on strike, Rachel knew that Leah and her friends were working very hard to get workers in other factories to support their cause as well.

"Rachel, you came!" Leah shouted as soon as Rachel stepped in the door. It was warm in the restaurant, and the smell of food made

Rachel hungry.

"Have you invited me for lunch?" Rachel asked, hoping she would get a good meal.

"No," Leah said, shaking her head. "I need you to take these handbills to Union Square and hand them out to everyone you see."

Rachel looked at the papers in her sister's hand. The words looked foreign to her. She knew that they were not written in English, Russian, or Yiddish—the languages she could read.

"What does this say?" Rachel asked.

"I have no time to explain now," Leah said, pushing her out the door. "I'll see you at home for supper."

"And thank you," Rachel muttered, once she got out on the street.

Rachel walked over to Union Square. She really admired Leah, and the work she was doing for the union. She was following her own advice and speaking up for what she thought was right. Perhaps by handing out these handbills, Rachel could show her sister that she was a fighter, too.

When she reached Union Square, she saw other men and women handing out handbills to the people on the street. In the middle of the crowd, Rachel noticed a young boy, with a cap pulled over his eyes. Rachel walked closer to the figure.

"Antonio?" she said to the boy.

The boy looked up. "Oh, hello, Rachel," Antonio said. "I guess your sister recruited you, too."

Rachel nodded her head. "Yes, she shoved these papers in my hand and told me to come up here and give them out. There's just one problem, though."

"I don't know what they say," they said together, and started to laugh.

"Here, let me look at yours," Antonio said, taking the handbill from Rachel. "Why, this is written in Italian!"

Rachel took a paper from Antonio's pile. "And this is written in Yiddish!" she exclaimed.

Now Rachel was able to understand what the handbills said. They announced a meeting that was to be held that night at Cooper Union Hall to discuss the possibility of a general strike by all the shirtwaist workers.

"How boring," Antonio said, yawning. "Why are our sisters so concerned with this anyway?"

"Because the factory owners aren't treating the workers well," Rachel explained.

"So?" Antonio said. "That's just part of working, isn't it?"

Rachel shook her head. "No. You don't understand what it's like. You've never worked in a factory."

"That's true," Antonio agreed.

"I have an idea," Rachel said. "Let's ask our sisters if we can go to the meeting tonight."

"That's a terrific idea," Antonio said. "Maybe a fight will break out. It'll be fun!" he said, smacking a fist into his palm.

Suddenly, Rachel was wondering what she was getting herself into.

That night, Cooper Union Hall was crowded. Workers overflowed into Beethoven Hall, Manhattan Lyceum, and other meeting rooms. People spoke to the crowd in English and Yiddish, some in favor of the strike, others against it.

Rachel shifted her tired feet. She had been standing for almost two hours now, crushed among hundreds of bodies.

"I guess this wasn't such a good idea," Antonio said, stifling a yawn. "I'm practically falling asleep on my feet."

Rachel smiled. "I know what you mean."

Just then, a teenager approached the speaker's platform. Rachel gasped. "I know her. That's Clara Lemlich. She was on the picket line with Leah." The girl began speaking in Yiddish.

"Rachel," Antonio whispered, "I can't understand what she's saying."

"I'll translate for you," Rachel volunteered.

"I am a working girl, one of those who are on strike against intolerable conditions. I am tired of listening to speakers who talk in general terms," Rachel translated. "I guess she means that no one here is getting to the point. She's one of the people who's on strike now, and she thinks that everyone should strike. She's tired of hearing people talk in circles."

"I'm tired of listening to the speakers altogether," Antonio whispered.

"Ssh!" Rachel said. "I can't hear her. She's saying that we're here to decide whether all the factories should go on strike. And she thinks a strike should be called now."

Upon hearing the girl's words, the crowd went wild. Everyone was shouting to strike.

People waved hats, canes, handkerchiefs, or whatever else was in their hands. The shouting and cheering went on for almost five minutes.

When the meeting was over, Rachel and Antonio followed the crowd out into the street. The air was cold, but in their excitement, they barely felt it. The workers shouted, for all to hear, that they were on strike.

"Come on," Antonio said. "I've had enough of this. Let's go." He grabbed Rachel's hand and pulled her through the crowd.

Rachel felt torn. She wanted to stay with her sister and the other strikers, but she wanted to go with Antonio, too. Then she decided that she had shown enough support for one day.

A few blocks away, Rachel shook her head to clear it, and the sounds of shouting died away in the cool night air.

"I'll walk you home," Antonio said.

As they were nearing her neighborhood, Rachel heard a dog barking. The barks turned into howls, and the howls into cries.

"Let's go see where that's coming from," Rachel suggested.

Rachel and Antonio followed the sound into a back alley. There, lit by the moon, was a little brown and white scruffy dog. Quietly, they approached the animal. The dog growled, and bared his teeth.

"Come on, puppy," Rachel called, holding out her hand. "Don't be afraid."

The dog ran up to them, sniffed their fingers, and then licked them.

Antonio laughed. "It looks like we've found a friend."

"He's probably starving," Rachel said.

Antonio ran over to a garbage bin, and fished out a stale piece of bread. The dog swallowed it in one bite. Then Antonio took an old box and filled it with newspapers. "There, I've made a home for him."

"It Looks Like We've Found a Friend"

The dog crawled into the box, and curled up in the papers. He looked at Rachel and Antonio and gave a little yelp.

"Sounds like he's thanking us," Rachel said.

Antonio shrugged. "We haven't done much. We just gave him a piece of old bread and something to keep him warm for the night."

"But that's a lot," Rachel said. "This poor dog doesn't have anyone to care for him. I have an idea. Let's come back tomorrow and see how he's doing. We can make him our secret project."

"Yes," Antonio agreed. "Our sisters have their special project, and now we have ours."

CHAPTER SIX
"We've Got Work to Do"

The next day, Rachel rose early. Leah was already gone. Rachel walked over to the sink to splash some cold water on her face. She sighed. She longed to live in an apartment that had a toilet inside, instead of in the hallway outside. Some day, she thought, some day. She sighed again, and locked her dreams away in her head.

As Rachel dressed, she wondered what it would be like to live the life of one of the characters in her books. Oh, how she'd enjoy going to school and playing outside with her friends, and not worrying about having to help support her family. Then she smiled. At least I'll get to play with the dog today, she thought.

She reached up into the cupboard and took out a piece of bread. Tearing the bread in half, she stuffed one piece in her mouth, the other in her pocket.

Rachel tiptoed through the living room, where her two brothers lay sleeping. Her little sister still slept in her parents' room. Quietly, she opened the front door, and stepped out into the dingy hallway.

Once outside, Rachel looked around at the soot-covered buildings and the rusting fire escapes, and smiled. Today, for some reason, everything looked beautiful. She took a deep breath, and twirled around, letting her dress and petticoat catch the breeze. Then she ran to the place where she and Antonio had left the dog.

"What took you so long?" Antonio demanded, as Rachel entered the dark alley.

The dog ran up to her and licked her fingers. "I got here as soon as I could," Rachel said.

"So," Antonio said, "what did you bring?"

Rachel proudly pulled out the piece of bread from her pocket.

Antonio stared at it. "That's all?" he asked.

Rachel's face reddened. "Why, yes. This is all I could manage to get out of the house. What did you bring?"

Antonio unwrapped a piece of newspaper. Inside was a selection of fruit, vegetables, and even a few pieces of pastries.

Rachel's stomach began to growl. Oh, to have such a feast for myself! she thought.

"Looks good, doesn't it?" Antonio said.

Rachel nodded. "Where did you get all that food?"

"I work with my father peddling food on

Mott Street," Antonio said. "These fruits and vegetables weren't sold yesterday, so I took them for the dog. And the pastries I got on Elizabeth Street."

"Your family must never be hungry, then," Rachel said.

Antonio laughed. "No, there have been plenty of days when there wasn't enough food on the table. We try to sell all of the food on our cart every day. The food we don't sell is just like lost money," he explained.

"I see," Rachel said. "Well, let's give this food to our dog. He really looks hungry."

"And so do you," Antonio said with a grin, tossing her a pastry. "You didn't think these were for the dog, did you?"

"I guess I did, but I'm glad I was wrong. These look delicious," Rachel said as she bit into the pastry.

"So what kind of work do you do now that the factory is on strike?" Antonio asked Rachel after they had finished the rest of the pastries.

"I help my mother with her sewing. She makes clothes for some of the people in the neighborhood."

"Sounds exciting," Antonio said, rolling his eyes.

Rachel shrugged. "I really don't have a choice. My family needs the money."

"If you could do anything you wanted," Antonio said, "what would you do?"

"I would go to school," Rachel answered promptly. "I loved school in Russia, and I used to like it here, too. I really want to become a teacher some day, not a seamstress. But as soon as I turned eleven, Papa sent me off to work."

"On my eleventh birthday, my father made me start work, too," Antonio said, shaking his head. "Believe it or not, I also liked school."

Rachel was surprised to discover how similar Antonio's story was to hers.

"I still try to read as much as I can," Antonio continued. "I love taking a book out to read on the fire escape."

Rachel smiled. "So do I."

"Maybe you could save up some money to go to night school one day," Antonio suggested. "That's what I'm trying to do. My father lets me keep some of the money I earn."

"That would be nice," Rachel agreed, "but how would I do that? Every penny I earn goes to Papa. He would never let me keep anything."

Antonio thought for a moment. "I know— you could peddle."

"Peddle?" Rachel said. "What? How?"

"That's simple. I can teach you how to do it. And I could give you some fruits and vegetables to sell," Antonio said.

"I will not take charity," Rachel said proudly.

"I know," Antonio said. "You can pay me back with your earnings." He grabbed

Rachel's hand and pulled her out of the alley.

They ran over to Mott Street, where men, women, and children peddled their wares. Rachel saw horse-drawn wagons and push-carts filled with colorful mountains of fresh fruits and vegetables. Peddlers were yelling out prices, and shoppers were pushing at each other in order to reach the freshest piece of fruit or the crispiest-looking vegetables. To Rachel, the scene looked just like the ones on Hester and Orchard Streets, where she shopped.

"You're late!" a man scolded Antonio in heavily accented English. He had dark eyes and a mop of curly dark hair. Although Rachel could hear him talking, she could not see his mouth, which was hidden by a big bushy moustache.

"Sorry, Papa," Antonio said. "I've brought a friend along to help me. This is…"

"I don't care who you've brought," he interrupted. "Just get to work." With that, he pushed a cart at Antonio, and stormed away.

"Let's go, Rachel," Antonio said. "We've got work to do."

Antonio pushed his cart into the middle of the crowded street. "Get your fresh vegetables, here! Get your fresh fruit!" he sang out.

Rachel covered her ears. "Do you have to yell so loudly?" she asked.

"Of course," Antonio said. "How else do you think I'll be able to get people's attention? This is your first lesson in peddling. Watch."

Although Rachel appreciated what Antonio was trying to do for her, she didn't think she'd be able to peddle. She had a hard time even speaking to people. Now he wanted her to scream in the middle of the street?

"Pay attention, Rachel," Antonio said, pushing his cart between a crowd of people. "Fresh vegetables, fresh fruit!" he called.

A woman stopped at his cart. She picked out some food, and Antonio wrapped it in newspaper. Soon, more women and young girls stopped to buy fruit and vegetables from Antonio.

"This isn't so hard, is it?" Antonio asked Rachel when most of his food was sold.

Rachel shook her head.

"I have a few pieces left," Antonio said, pointing to his cart. "Now you try."

"Oh, no," Rachel said. "I could never peddle here."

"Why not?" Antonio looked confused.

"Because this is the Italian neighborhood. I don't belong here," Rachel explained.

"Then let's go where you'll feel more comfortable," Antonio said. "Only we won't tell my father. It'll be our secret."

Soon Rachel and Antonio were standing in the middle of Hester Street. Here, as on Mott Street, the area was crowded with peddlers and shoppers. Horses pulled wagons filled with chickens, eggs, clothing, pots and pans, and anything else worthy of being sold.

"Go ahead," Antonio said, motioning to

Rachel to stand behind the cart.

"Fruits, vegetables," Rachel said in a small voice.

"I can't even hear you," Antonio said. "How do you expect to get the attention of this crowd?"

"Fruits, vegetables," Rachel said a little louder.

"That's not good enough. I want you to really yell. Pretend you're very angry."

Rachel didn't want to tell Antonio that she rarely got angry. And when she did, she would never yell. She took a deep breath. "Fruit, vegetables! Get your fruit and vegetables here!" she yelled. Her voice echoed in her ears. She did it!

A woman rushed up to Rachel. Then another, and another. Each time someone bought something, Rachel dropped the coins into her pocket.

Soon the pushcart was empty. Antonio smiled. "You did a good job, Rachel.

Welcome to the world of peddling."

Rachel gave some of the money to Antonio. Then she walked home, the remaining coins jingling in her pocket and visions of a better future filling her head. She *could* get what she wanted. Things *could* be better.

CHAPTER SEVEN
"Let's Get Her!"

"A peddler? My daughter is a peddler?" Rachel's father yelled as he walked in the door that evening.

Rachel stayed in the kitchen, concentrating on the potato she was peeling.

"Have you nothing to say, daughter?" Mr. Boganovitch stormed into the kitchen.

Rachel looked up at her papa. His brown eyes looked stormy. "I was trying to earn some extra money," Rachel stammered.

"No daughter of mine will be a peddler! I don't care how bad things get," he shouted, pounding his chest. "I was a proud man in Russia, an educated man!"

"But you'll let her work in terrible conditions in the factory. Why is that, Papa?" Rachel heard Leah say.

"And you," Mr. Boganovitch whirled around to face Leah, "I will have none of your back talk. It is bad enough that you parade around outside fighting for these, these rights as you call them, and this union of yours. But I will not have a child of mine peddle!"

"Now, Rachel," he continued, "since you did work today, give me your earnings." He held his hand out in front of her. "But I do not want to hear of this peddling business again. Understand?"

Rachel stared at him. She could not let her father take this money from her. "No, Papa!" she shouted. "You do not understand."

Rachel watched her father closely as she spoke. How was he going to react to this sudden outburst?

"I too want to be educated," Rachel said quickly, not giving her father a chance to respond. "I gave you the money from the factory, and I help Mama with the sewing. This money is for me. I am saving up for night school."

Papa's eyes narrowed and, slowly, a smile began to form on his lips. "So, my quiet one speaks out," he said. "Very well, you may keep your earnings. But a peddler...Well, maybe Leah is right. How much worse can it be to peddle than to slave in a factory for fourteen hours a day? All right, Rachel, you have my permission. But this work must not interfere with your household responsibilities."

"Yes, Papa," Rachel said with relief. She had done it!

That night, after the last dish was cleaned, and every crumb was swept from the floor,

Rachel picked up a book and climbed out onto the fire escape. The moon was out, casting its brilliant light on the black iron bars.

A child laughed in the distance. A dog yipped. Rachel sighed, and looked up at the sky. The stars were so bright. Today she had not let her sister protect her; she had stood up to Papa. Maybe deep down she was a fighter, like Leah.

It was Friday, the day that Rachel always helped her mother with the shopping. That night was the beginning of the Sabbath, and Mrs. Boganovitch, like other Jewish women, always prepared a special meal.

Rachel and her mother pushed through the crowded streets and chose a plump chicken and some vegetables for the soup. When the hour began to grow late, Mrs. Boganovitch asked Rachel to finish the shopping and meet her at home.

Rachel purchased some herring for the family's Saturday evening meal from the fish man. "Do you have any squashed fish?" she asked him.

The peddler gave her a puzzled look. "I don't get many requests for squashed fish," he said.

Rachel smiled. "But that's the only kind my friend will eat. Besides, won't it cost less?"

The man laughed. "Yes, young lady. You are right." He wrapped up two fish in newspaper and handed them to her.

Once the shopping was completed, Rachel rushed over to the alley. She knew the dog would love the treat she had brought.

"Here, dog," Rachel called out.

"That's no name for a dog," she heard someone say. She looked around and saw Antonio sitting on top of a garbage can.

"You startled me," Rachel said.

"Well, who else do you think would be in this alley?" Antonio asked.

Rachel shrugged. "I don't know. What are

you doing here?"

"I've been sitting here trying to think of a name for our dog," he said. "And I've come up with a great one. Wolf."

"Wolf?" Rachel repeated. "He looks nothing like a wolf. Wolves are fierce, and our dog is gentle. No, we need something more unusual."

"So what's your suggestion?" Antonio asked.

Rachel put down her parcels and thought a moment. "Sebahka," she said.

"Sebahka?" Antonio repeated. "It sounds interesting, but what does it mean?"

"It means dog in Russian," Rachel explained.

"I like it," Antonio said.

"Look what we have here!" a gruff voice called out.

Rachel looked to one end of the alley. Two tall boys stood there. Their dirty clothes were tattered, and the caps on their heads were worn backwards. But what concerned Rachel the most was what they were holding in their hands—baseball bats.

"What's in the bags, little girl?" one of the bullies asked.

"N-nothing," Rachel said.

The boys moved closer. "It smells like food to me," one boy said. "And we're hungry."

"Leave us alone!" Antonio said, jumping down from the garbage can.

"So you have a bodyguard," one of the bullies said with a laugh. "I don't think he'll do you any good, though. Come on boys. Let's get her."

Rachel turned to the other end of the alley and saw two more boys standing there. Her heart began to race. They were surrounded, and there was no way out!

CHAPTER EIGHT
"We'll Have a Better Life"

Suddenly, Rachel heard a loud growl. One of the hoodlums looked around. "What was that?" he asked.

"It's just a stray mutt," another boy answered. "Let's get the food before he does."

The four boys took a step closer. Just then, Sebahka leaped from his box and ran toward the attackers, barking and growling fiercely.

"It's a mad dog!" one of the boys cried.

Sebahka took hold of a leg of one boy's

pants with his teeth and began twisting it around. The boy frantically tried to get loose.

"Come on, Rachel," Antonio said urgently. "Let's go!"

"But they have bats," Rachel said, her eyes transfixed on the scene that was unfolding before her. "Sebahka could get hurt."

"I think he can take care of himself." Antonio watched Sebahka dodge the swinging bat and run away.

Rachel grabbed her bags, and she and Antonio fled the alley, unnoticed by the hoodlums.

After running as fast as they could for a few blocks, Rachel and Antonio stopped.

"That was a close one," Antonio said in between breaths.

Rachel bent over, placed the bags on the sidewalk, and put her hands on her knees. "I know what you mean," she agreed. She looked up. The daylight was beginning to fade. Soon it would be sundown, and the

Sabbath would begin.

"It's getting late," Rachel said. "I must get home. The Sabbath will be starting soon."

"Sabbath?" Antonio said. "That's on Sunday. Today's only Friday."

Rachel laughed. "Maybe for you. But for Jewish people, like me, the Sabbath begins at sundown on Friday."

"I see," Antonio said, nodding his head.

"I have an idea," Rachel said. "Why don't you come to my house for dinner? Then you can see how we celebrate."

"I don't know," Antonio said. "That might not be a good idea."

"Sure it is," Rachel said with a smile. "Run home and tell your parents where you'll be. Meet me at my house in half an hour." She scribbled down her address on a piece of paper and handed it to Antonio.

"Where have you been?" Rachel's mother asked when she walked in the door.

"Oh, Mama," Rachel said. "It was terrible."

"What is it, child?"

"Some boys tried to rob me. They tried to take my packages."

"Are you all right?" her mother asked.

Rachel nodded. "A boy helped me," she said. "And I invited him to dinner tonight."

"Bless him," Mrs. Boganovitch said. "He is welcome in our house. Thank goodness you weren't hurt. Now go get ready for dinner."

Rachel turned away and smiled. That was simple, she thought.

A little while later, Antonio knocked on the door. "So you're the young man who rescued my daughter," Rachel's father boomed as they walked into the living room.

Antonio raised his eyebrows and looked at Rachel. She winked at him.

"Yes, sir," Antonio said.

"What is your name, son?" Mr. Boganovitch asked.

"My name is Antonio Russo."

"Russo," Rachel's father repeated, looking Antonio over. He knew that was an Italian name.

"It's time for dinner," Mrs. Boganovitch called out.

Antonio followed Rachel into the kitchen, where he was introduced to the rest of the family. They stood around a beautifully set table. A crisp white tablecloth hung over it, and the utensils and plates had a special glow. A vase with fresh cut flowers stood in the center, with candles on either side of it.

Mrs. Boganovitch lit the two candles. She moved her hands around in a circular motion and placed them over her face. Then she said a prayer in a language Antonio did not understand.

"That was Hebrew," Rachel whispered, when her mother had finished.

Next, Mr. Boganovitch lifted up a glass of wine, and recited another Hebrew prayer.

After that, he cut a twisted loaf of bread, reciting still another prayer.

"That bread is called challah," Rachel explained. "Now that my father has said the prayers, we can eat."

And eat they did. Antonio could not believe how much food they had—soup, roasted chicken, potato pudding, and vegetables. He wished he could eat the chicken, but he was Catholic and Catholics were not supposed to eat meat on Fridays. But he ate the potato pudding, the vegetables, and two thick slices of challah. Everything was delicious.

"Come on," Rachel said to Antonio after they had finished dinner. "I want to show you something."

She crawled out the window onto the fire escape. "This is where I go to hide," Rachel explained. "No one else in the family comes out here except me."

Antonio looked around. "I wish my fire escape faced the back. When I sit on mine, the whole world can see me."

"Yes, but you can see the world, too," Rachel said with a laugh.

"That was a good dinner," Antonio said. "Do you always eat like that?"

Rachel shook her head. "Only on Friday nights," she said. "And now that Leah and I aren't working at the factory, the family has to eat less during the week to save up for the Sabbath meal."

"I wish we could always have meals like that," Antonio said. "I'm tired of going hungry."

"I know what you mean," Rachel said. "When I was a little girl in Russia, I heard Papa telling Mama that in America things were plentiful. That we'd never have to worry about anything. And then we come here to live in a crowded tenement."

"So things were better in Russia?" Antonio asked.

"Well, we certainly had more money,"

Rachel said. "But our village was always being attacked because we were all Jewish. The attacks were called pogroms, and a lot of people were killed. That is why we left."

"I don't understand," Antonio said. "People hated you because you're Jewish?"

Rachel nodded her head. "It's terrible to think about, isn't it?"

They sat in silence for a few minutes. "One day we'll get out of here, Rachel," Antonio said. "We'll have a better life. You'll see. You'll see."

CHAPTER NINE
"Perhaps You Can Come and Visit Me Some Day"

In February Rachel and Leah returned to work at the Triangle Shirtwaist Company. Although a lot of other shirtwaist workers had gotten what they had demanded during the strike, the workers at the Triangle factory did not reach an agreement with the owners.

"How can you go back to work if you have lost?" Rachel asked Leah. "The owners are still going to lock the doors, and the fire escapes still don't work. And they haven't agreed to give us fair pay or shorter working hours."

"It's true, Rachel. We lost," Leah said. "But we worked hard, and a lot of other people won. Besides, this was the first time that women really spoke out and were heard."

"I still don't understand," Rachel said. "Was it worth all the trouble?"

Leah nodded her head. "Yes, Rachel. We convinced workers in other factories to go on strike, too. And a lot of them got what they asked for. We haven't given up hope here yet. One day we'll get what we want."

Rachel was exhausted after the day's work. She pushed open the factory doors and spotted Antonio across the street. She started to walk over to him, but noticed that he was with some of his friends. Now that the strike was over, was their friendship over, too?

"Rachel!" Antonio called. "Over here!"

Rachel breathed a sigh of relief, and walked over to Antonio.

"See you later," he called to his friends. "You look tired," he said to Rachel.

Rachel nodded. "I had forgotten how many hours I worked there," she said.

"I have something to tell you, Rachel," Antonio said.

"What is it?" Rachel looked worried.

"My family is moving. We're going to Brooklyn," Antonio said. "My father said we'll have a better life there. Our apartment will be bigger, and there are lots of trees there, too. I've written down the name of the place where you can buy the fruits and vegetables you need to peddle. They'll tell you where you can get a pushcart, too." Antonio handed her a slip of paper.

Rachel crumpled up the paper and shoved it in her pocket. "Antonio," she cried, "how can you leave?"

"I thought you might be happy for me,"

Antonio said.

"Well I'm not!" Rachel said. "Good-bye, Antonio Russo. Have a nice life!" With that, she ran down the street, leaving Antonio standing on the cold pavement staring after her.

When Rachel got home, she headed straight for the fire escape. Why did I act that way? she thought. Antonio was right, I should be happy for him. Instead, I acted like a jealous child. She shoved her hands into her pockets, and her fingers touched the piece of paper that Antonio had given her. She pulled it out, placed it on her lap, and tried to smooth out the wrinkles. How could I have been so mean to my friend? Rachel thought.

Then Rachel had an idea. She jumped up, ran into the living room, and pulled out the basket of scrap material. Sitting down behind the sewing machine, she began sewing the pieces together. When she was finished she grabbed the long piece of cloth, and ran out.

Rachel raced over to the alley and found Sebahka. She ruffled his fur and tied the cloth around his neck. It made a beautiful bow. Then she and the dog headed over to Mulberry Street.

When she reached Antonio's tenement, she saw him sitting on the fire escape.

"What are you doing here?" he asked. "I thought you already said good-bye."

"I was thinking," Rachel said, "that you should take Sebahka with you. After all, you said there were trees in Brooklyn."

Antonio smiled, and climbed down from his perch. "Thank you, Rachel," he said. "But I have nothing to give you. All my things have been packed away."

"That's all right," Rachel said. "You've already given me something—you've shown me a way to earn the money I need to go to night school." She fished the slip of paper out of her pocket and showed it to him.

"You know, Rachel," Antonio said.

"Brooklyn isn't that far away. Maybe you can come and visit me—and Sebahka."

Rachel smiled and nodded her head. She looked around her. The street lamps were lit and the stars were twinkling in the sky above the gray and dreary tenements. Yes, someday she too would move from this neighborhood, but she would never leave her memories behind.

Orchard Street, 1898, The Byron Collection, Museum of the City of New York

The Lower East Side of New York City was a busy, growing place at the turn of the century. Here, merchants and shoppers crowd Orchard Street in pre-automobile days.

Even though Rachel Boganovitch is a fictional character, many girls just like her lived and worked on the Lower East Side of New York City in the early 1900s. Families came to America from countries like Russia, Germany, and Italy, seeking a better life for themselves. Unfortunately, most of these immigrants ended up living in crowded tenements and working in oppressive sweatshops.

One of the most popular garments made in the sweatshops was the shirtwaist. It sold in such great quantities that it kept the large factories in which it was made busy six days a week. The largest of the New York shirtwaist manufacturers was the Triangle Shirtwaist Company, which employed more than five hundred people, most of them young immigrant women.

Work conditions at the Triangle factory were dismal. Crowded, unsanitary, and unsafe, the shop offered the women who worked in it only long hours and low wages. In 1908, after the Triangle workers went on strike to protest the conditions, the factory's owners allowed some of the workers to join a company union. Those workers were

Immigrants in big cities often found themselves living in crowded, dirty one- or two-room flats like this one.

fired within a year, however, and working conditions remained miserable.

In September 1909 about 200 Triangle employees went on strike again. This was the strike during which Leah was arrested in the story. This small strike led to a general strike of about 20,000 shirtwaist workers in December 1909. But, as we found out in the story, the 20,000 shirtwaist workers' two-month strike didn't much help the Triangle factory workers. It took the Triangle fire to focus attention on the need for labor reform and labor laws that would guarantee worker safety and limit the length of the working day.

More about...
The Triangle Shirtwaist Fire

On March 25, 1911, disaster struck the Triangle Shirtwaist Company. Black smoke poured out of the eighth floor windows of the Asch Building, where the factory was located. Soon, orange and yellow flames were also visible. A passerby looked up at the building and saw a bundle of cloth fall from one of the windows. Then the people on the street heard screams. The bundle was not made of cloth — it was a young girl who had jumped from the window, fleeing the fire inside.

Horse-drawn fire engines raced to the

Headquarters of the Shirt Waist Strikers: Miss Drier and Secretary. *Museum of the City of NY. Gift of Henry Bland.*

With little experience or guidance, the organizers of the shirtwaist strike managed to pull together one of the first and most important steps in labor reform.

burning building, and the fire ladders were raised. But the ladders only reached up to the sixth floor, and the fire had already reached the ninth floor. The firemen aimed their hoses up at the burning building and tried to extinguish the fire.

The fire was burning out of control. Most workers on the eighth floor crowded into the elevators or onto the fire escape or the stairs. Those on the tenth floor, warned by telephone, also crammed into the elevators or fled to the roof, where they were led to safety by New York University law students from the building next door.

Workers on the ninth floor were not so fortunate. Never alerted by telephone, they were trapped. Some tried to escape through the stairway exit but found the door locked. Some ran to the fire escape, but it quickly broke under their weight, sending the men and women tumbling to the ground below. Many workers leapt from windows to evade the flames, choosing the risk of injury over burning to death. Some made it to life nets held by firemen, but the nets failed as they were torn by the force of two and three bodies hitting them at the same time.

Of the 500 men and women who worked on the eighth, ninth, and tenth floors of the Asch Building, 146 (mostly women and young girls) died in the fire.

After the Fire

The people of New York City were outraged after the Triangle Shirtwaist Company fire. Many protest meetings were held. One of the largest meetings took place on April 2, 1911, at the Metropolitan Opera House. It was sponsored by the Women's Trade Union League. Speaker after speaker called for stricter factory inspection laws and safer working conditions.

On April 5, the mayor of New York City, William Gaynor, ordered that seven unidentified victims of the fire be buried at the Evergreen Cemetery in Brooklyn. On the same day, a memorial parade was held in Manhattan. About 100,000 workers marched in a procession up Fifth Avenue, with hundreds of thousands looking on.

The Investigation

The owners of the Triangle Shirtwaist Company, Isaac Harris and Max Blanck, were charged with first and second degree manslaughter. The prosecutors claimed that the factory doors were kept locked during the day, thereby contributing to the deaths. The jury, however, did not find the men guilty because the jurors concluded that Harris and Blanck did not know that the doors were locked.

The people of New York City were furious over this verdict, and many more protests took place.

Out of the Ashes

In 1911, two groups were formed to inspect safety standards in factories. The Bureau of Fire Prevention was established by New York City, and the Factory Investigating Commission was formed by the New York State legislature.

The Commission found unsafe working conditions in many factories across New York State. As a result, thirty-three labor laws were passed in 1914 to help protect workers.

To Learn More about the Labor Movement and the Triangle Shirtwaist Fire, Check Out...

Goldin, Barbara Diamond. *Fire! The Beginnings of the Labor Movement.* [New York: Viking, 1992.]

Kent, Zachary. *The Story of the Triangle Factory Fire.* [Chicago: The Children's Press, Inc., 1989.]

Naden, Corinne J. *The Triangle Shirtwaist Fire.* [New York: Franklin Watts, Inc., 1971.]

Wertheimer, Barbara Mayer. *We Were There: The Story of Working Women in America.* [New York: Pantheon Books, 1977.]

Other books in the STORIES OF THE STATES series

Drums at Saratoga*
American Dreams*
by Lisa Banim

Golden Quest*
by Bonnie Bader

Fire in the Valley
Mr. Peale's Bones
Voyage of the Half Moon*
by Tracey West

Forbidden Friendship
by Judy Eichler Weber

Children of Flight Pedro Pan
by Maria Armengol Acierno

A Message for General Washington
by Vivian Schurfranz

*Available in paperback

If you are interested in ordering other STORIES OF THE STATES books, please call Silver Moon Press at our **toll free** number (800) 874-3320 or send an order to:

Silver Moon Press
160 Fifth Avenue, Suite 622
New York, NY 10010

All hardcovers are $13.95 and all paperbacks are $5.95. (Please add 8% shipping, or a minimum of $4.50)